Pa

T0153284

A short story about reciprocity

Louisa Thomsen Brits

With photographs by Jim Marsden and artwork by Linda Felcey

Book Co

*For my children Bella, Milo,
Manu and Taya and the paths
that they will tread*

Published by
The Do Book Company 2018
Works in Progress Publishing Ltd
thedobook.co

This paperback edition published 2023

Text © Louisa Thomsen Brits 2018, 2023
Photography © Jim Marsden 2018
Artwork © Linda Felcey 2018

The right of Louisa Thomsen Brits
to be identified as author of this
work has been asserted by her in
accordance with the Copyright,
Designs and Patents Act 1988

A CIP catalogue record for this book
is available from the British Library

ISBN 978-1-914168-23-9

Designed by Ratiotype

Printed and bound by
OZGraf Print on Munken,
an FSC® certified paper

Preface

Why do we pick up a particular book? Or choose to write one? What draws us to explore one publication or path in favour of another, moving page by page, pace by pace, along the lines before us?

In reading, like walking, we lose and find ourselves. Both lift us beyond quotidian existence, shift our perspective, meet our longings, help us find expression and comfort, even prepare us for the unknown.

It's strange, sometimes, the way in which our artistic minds seem to be ahead of us, calling from a place with a clearer view, just out of sight. What are the impulses that drive us to create? How do we know what is expressing itself through and within us?

Two days after *Path* was published, walking at the
foot of the South Downs on an inland track that
leads from the old coach road to Charleston
Farmhouse, I found a chalk-white, heart-shaped
fossil — a sea urchin; its five-fold star radiating
from the past, reaching into the present moment.
A thunderstone for protection in tough times.
In my palm, it gleamed like a gift from the paths
that I tread and observe; a talisman to carry with
me when, a few weeks later, I was admitted to
hospital for a wholly unexpected mastectomy.

While I had been writing about moving through
mist and dark twists of briar and blackthorn,
a constellation of tumours had nested deep in the
tissue of my left breast, close to my heart — the
unexpressed finding form in my body, inviting me
to unravel a tangle of sorrow to a navigable thread.
It seems that in writing *Path*, I had unwittingly
given expression to some abiding truth beneath
the surface of my understanding.

Our poetic awareness exists in the realm of intuition
and insight. It's a way of perceiving and receiving
the world. All life takes place within one poetic space,
each being engaged in poiesis — a bringing forth
of something that didn't exist before. Each one an
expression of aliveness and the desire to flourish,
to reach out and connect. Each engaged in acts of
individual and collective meaning-making.

If a sense of enlivenment can be understood as poetic, then poetry can be experienced as a verb, and walking as motion and devotion; ways of attending to the inner and outer ecology of our lives and entering into communion with the whole community of beings. Both summon the joy of embodiment. From the body and its gestures, relationships grow.

Language, at its core, is a physical thing that can create a sensory experience in another person's mind and body. I wrote *Path* while walking. It's a mimetic account of a local walk; shaped according to its rhythms, from dawn to dusk. I didn't write it as a poem but made an attempt to capture, in patterned intensity of language, the rhythm, syntax and texture of the downland where I live and the characters that I encountered en route. I picked Sussex dialect words along the way, their sturdy roots entangled with the utterances of this place. In giving the narrative voice to the path itself, I hoped to invite the landscape to speak.

Instead of an account of a hero's journey of self to summit, I chose to gather impressions, to write a short story that might express the value of encounter, of call and response, registration and reciprocity.

I see now that *Path* is also a story about moving through uncertainty, prescient of my own journey through diagnosis and treatment of breast cancer. Since its publication in hardback, countless people have navigated the precariousness and pain of living through a pandemic. And, in response to lives circumscribed by lockdowns and fear, many thousands have taken up walking, entering into a new intimacy with the landscape of their lives; engaging with the particulars of home and their local neighbours, human and non-human.

My only brief for writing *Path* was to 'lead the reader from where they are, to where they want to be'. Paths are a well-worn trope, perhaps, but they represent the countless threads that connect us in a skein of interdependency and shared beingness. Anthropologist Tim Ingold speaks of 'wayfaring', a way of combining movement and attention. Life is lived *'along paths, not just in places,'* he says, and it's along paths, *'that people grow into a knowledge of the world around them, and describe this world in the stories they tell.'*

This book is itself an intersection of lives; a collaborative creation with fine artist Linda Felcey and photographer Jim Marsden, as we walked in rhythmic participation and creative conversation with each other and with the land.

In collaboration, we magnify and tend each other's spirit and nurture creative impulse. It was a privilege to work with Linda and Jim. In this culture of individualism, collaboration is vital and vitalising, a rare privilege. This felt like art-making as life itself. As Basho, the 17th-century Japanese haiku master, said, *'Real poetry, is to lead a beautiful life. To live poetry is better than to write it.'*

For as long as I can remember, I have walked to experience harmony with the earth and, in the words of Nan Shepherd, to *'know Being'*. In the years since *Path* was first published, I've felt compelled to consider a life of presence and participation rather than performance and productivity.

Walking returns us to the ground of our being. In a different way, illness does the same. *Humus*, the Latin word for soil or earth, and *humble* come from the same rich source. In nurturing a sense of humility, we foster connection and continuity.

Path is an invitation to wander and wonder; to experience radical openness and fidelity to the moment.

My hope is that this book suggests how we might attend to the world and reminds us how paths provide a sense of ongoingness amid the flux of our lives.

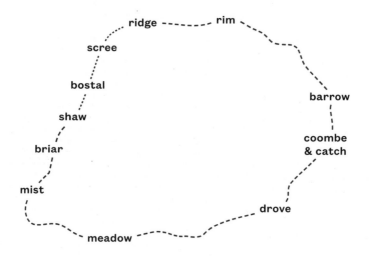

'Paths connect. This is their first duty
and their chief reason for being.'

Robert Macfarlane, *The Old Ways*

I am footfall and track,

trail and trace,

thread of passage and possibility,

invitation,

imprint of impulse,

a way-worn map of memory,

line of sign, scuff and shine

of shoe and shod,

cart-rut, groove, runnel and clod

as wheels

and seasons

and years roll by.

I am the pace and pause

of wayfarers,

wanderers,

drovers and dreamers,

dawdlers,

soldiers,

artists,

of ramblers and radicals,

poets and pilgrims.

In their tread, I follow their purpose

and fathom my own.

Each makes their mark

and leaves their wake

across these blunt hills of chalk,

    wind and shifting light.

Some I meet just once.

Others follow me again and again.

Before the day begins,

you are here

to braid your story to the ribbon of lives

      that pass this way.

I cast my milk-white, chalk-bright spell

and you pace a line of desire onto the grass.

Walk with me.

Together we will pattern the earth,
tracing the surface of the land.

As mist-shroud and low cloud

meet the soft-veiled truth of early morning,

step into stillness littered with flint and chaffinch song.

I feel the weight of uncertainty
carried on your shoulders.

Everything is edge-blurred, dew-clung, web-spun.

You strain to see
past cant and hedge
along the laine.

Yield to me
yield to instinct and chance.

Trust this twisted route through briar,
		bramble and purple-spined blackthorn
where blossom, light as snow,
		has scattered the promise of spring.

There, in the knotted dark, rests a soft
		mass of moss and feather titmouse nest.

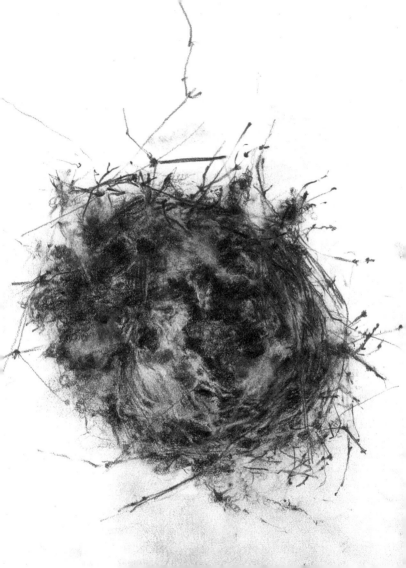

Pursue a track in the land, a train of thought

and I will draw you on and up,

over a trail of white stones and bruised stalks,

while the mist diffuses and reassembles your purpose,

rain-veiling and revealing our path.

I offer to make sense of the world,

to unravel tangle to intelligible thread,

I am your next natural step,

a silent, sinuous course stretching ahead of you,

from where you are now to where you hope to be.

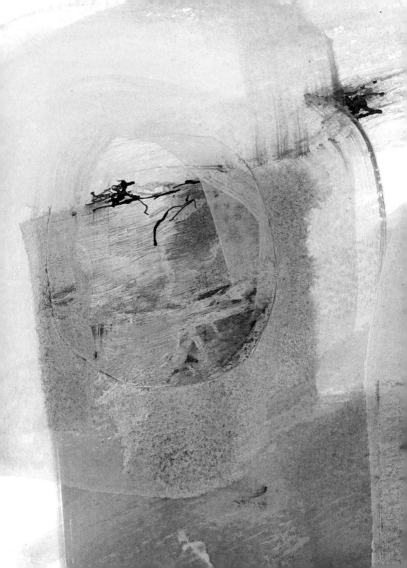

A sudden skylark, selved in song,
climbs up, up, up,
lifting matter and spirit,
silvering the waking world
with freshness,
dropping a string of bright notes
between you and the unexplored.

I am promise and purpose,

trail of flight.

Follow me

to the edge of a wood

and pause to find yourself in a chapel of slender trees.

Step into this silent shaw of oak and sycamore,

up scarp of bark, chalk-flake, mud and root-reach,

through shadow and light,

to meet yourself,

and tread me into being.

Along an aisle of crushed-flat leafmeal,

seams of chalk appear

and pale traces of your intention are revealed.

Hymns of light fall from the trees

as our vaulted canopy opens to clear sky.

Our path grows wider,

wilder.

Obscurity lifts to clarity as you follow my wilful course

up scrambly bostal,

over rill and rimple,

fists of thistle,

rutted sod.

Slip, step, slide, step

climbing a scree of resistance

to meet the terrain ahead.

Heavy-heeled,

footslog and tromp,

with quickening breath

and shortening step,

you stalk your purpose.

Up hill

steady climb,

traversing trampled ground and silverweed

we slowly rise

to nab and ridge

to meet a keeper of the beacon,

      remnant of woodland,

a wind-bent age-black hawthorn

twisting away from the slope

in a perpetual gust.

It speaks to you of quiet endurance.

In blue and spacious air,

crows — tar-black tricksters lit with life —

    dangle and birl.

Coat flaps fly out,

wings clap,

and you unfurl,

perched on the edge

of possibility,

balanced between

earth and sky,

a free and weightless identity

that lifts and flows over yellow gorse,

    dip and dung

to gather wild impulse.

Cast off your cares.

Let thought spool ahead of you

      across these close-cropped hills;

send out strong thread of being

      to stitch together self and earth.

Each footprint follows folds and seams,

tacking blocks of gentle stripes, stippled green,

bleached and winter-browned fields and fences.

Follow railway lines and ragged hedges

along wires, around dewponds, curves and shadows,

to sweep

with the breeze

up higher ground

into open sky, caressing clouds,

then on to circle the pale sun,

until everything is one vibrant tapestry.

I am prospect and progress.

Here you stride with long, strong, even pace

    and easy breath,

along rim and rise,

a single life

between infinite sky and sheltering ground,

walking your body into this moment,

measuring yourself against the earth,

moving towards a gradual sureness

one step

at

a time.

Stroll, stride,

steady beat

the pulse

of time

itself.

Steadfast course,

footing forwards,

pace by pace,

I carry you to a timeless place

where thoughts of past, present, and future

shapeshift,

and, wind-kissed,

you drift

flowing onwards, folding back,

along a luminous stream that spirals through

what lies unchanged beneath and within you.

Walking the bare spine of the hills,

you leave a path laid with light —

boots flecked white

    with flakes of early sea and sunshine,

the sediment of years,

scuffed from the chalk-bright realm

    beneath the turf.

Stand still. Look back
to see how far you have travelled.

Alive to the path behind and the path ahead,
no longer
chasing yourself in imagination
nor lagging behind,
you curve towards home.

circle slowly and the world delivers itself to you.

I am habit
I am balm.

Every step
the earth holds good.
Ebb and flow
of gentle breath.

Murmur of mind,
body and place.
Unwilled rhythm
and beating heart.

Moving to find stillness,
from dawn to dusk
between the mystery of the cosmos
and the music of stones,
you saunter into presence.

Walk
only walk
kiss the ground with your feet,
always arriving
into the here and now.

There is no destination,
nothing to do, to change, or mend but
wander with me to remember the land.

Stroll through weightless hours,
each step complete at every point along the way.

A fugitive feather floats lightly
to settle out of the wind in a plundered barrow.
Rest there
on a cushion of moss and sprung grass,
curled, cupped in sweet earth,
a grave-shallow, hollow-held home
right in the middle of the world,

like the countless shells,
always unfurling,
that litter the ground with their fragility,
each a delicate haven
where coiled darkness
unwinds into light
and ongoing life.

Sleep until the place inside you echoes
the space around you
and you carry everything you need,
into the truce of evening.

Walk into the land

through coombe and catch,

calm and free,

with late sun on your back,

held by banks of earth and buried passage,

gently herded

towards the place where you set out.

The slanting light carves shadows,

caresses the curves of the glittering reach,

and leaves a furrowed field lucent with life,

    flint-glint and imprint.

Everything is illuminated and itself

and you see that

I am not a single track but a glimmering web of ways.

I am paw print, tail-brush, spoor and smeuse,

wing-sweep, feather, foil and fur.

Tracks of deer, sheep, rabbit, pheasant and fox

dust

skim

stroke

touch

hop and brush

casting traces across our shared terrain.

These trails of encounter,

glimpse of kin,

transform your solitude to multitude.

Each walks their own path.

Each path connects,

criss-crossing in a rustling network,

our common language of passage and presence,

looped and knotted in a bright skein of reciprocity

holding the many lives that intersect your own.

Tread lightly

through shared stories shaped by seasons,

the song of the landscape

that belongs to all.

You stand in an intimate lattice of paths,

laced in plenitude,

and know that you are not alone.

Together we reach outwards and onwards,

each gleaming life intertwined

in the endless and eternal ceremony of being.

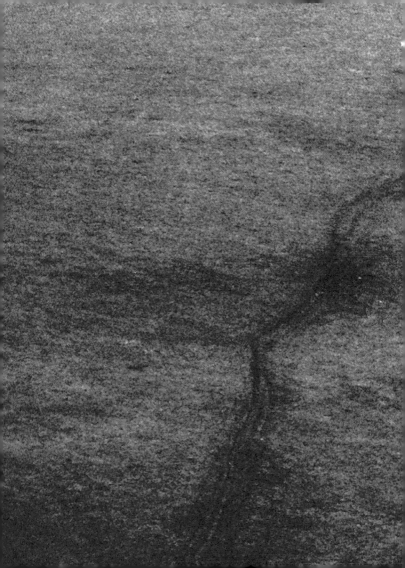

Glossary

Source: Most of the words below are vocabulary of place unique to Sussex and many are drawn from the selection of Robert Macfarlane's growing word-hoard that is to be found in his book *Landmarks*.

17   *cant* – corner of a field
     laine – open tract of arable land at the foot of the Downs

24   *shaw* – a small wood on a hillside
     scarp – steep face of a hill

27   *leafmeal* – tree's 'cast self', disintegrating as fallen leaves (Gerard Manley Hopkins)

30   *bostal* – pathway up a hill, generally very steep
     scree – mass of small stones and pebbles that forms on a steep mountain slope

33   *nab* – summit of a hill
     beacon – conspicuous hill with long sightlines from its summit (suitable for a beacon-fire)

35   *birl* – spin or whirl

50   *barrow* – an ancient burial mound

52   *combe, coombe* – valley: in the chalk-lands of southern England, a hollow or valley on the flank of a hill, or a steep short valley running up from the sea coast

52   *reach* – level, uninterrupted stretch of water on a river

55   *spoor* – the track or scent of an animal
     smeuse – a gap in the base of a hedge made by the regular passage of a small animal
     foil – tracks of deer on grass

56   *skein* – a length of thread or yarn, loosely coiled and knotted. An element that forms part of a complex or complicated whole

Bibliography
(alphabetical by author)

In Praise of Walking
Thomas A. Clark
(Artworks)

The Path to the Sea
Thomas A. Clark
(Arc Publications)

*Poems and Prose of
Gerard Manley Hopkins*
Selected and Edited
by W. H. Gardner
(Penguin)

A Philosophy of Walking
Frédéric Gros
(Verso)

*Call me by My
True Names:
The Collected Poems
of Thich Nhat Hanh*
(Parallax Press)

Braiding Sweetgrass
Robin Wall Kimmerer
(Milkweed Editions)

Earth Pilgrim
Satish Kumar
(Green Books)

Walking The Line
Richard Long,
Paul Moorhouse
and Denise Hooker
(Thames and Hudson)

The Old Ways
Robert Macfarlane
(Hamish Hamilton)

Landmarks
Robert Macfarlane
(Hamish Hamilton)

On Trails
Robert Moor
(Aurum Press)

Pathlands
Peter Owen Jones
(Rider)

*Reality Is Not What
It Seems*
Carlo Rovelli
(Penguin)

The Living Mountain
Nan Shepherd
(Canongate)

Wanderlust
Rebecca Solnit
(Granta)

In Pursuit of Spring
Edward Thomas
(Little Toller Books)

Walking
Henry David Thoreau

*Richard Long Selected
Statements & Interviews*
Edited by Ben Tufnell
(Haunch of Venison)

Six Facets of Light
Anne Wroe
(Jonathan Cape)

Author's note and acknowledgments

Paths, words and the rhythm and ritual of walking help me to navigate myself and the world.

Path is a collaboration, a reflection of friendship and an invaluable creative dialogue with artist Linda Felcey and photographer Jim Marsden. Thank you both for walking with me in all weathers.

Thank you to Lynda Edwardes-Evans for convincing me that I should stay the course of a writer, for your friendship and invaluable editorial support.

A book, like a path, is an accumulation of the steps and stories of all those who have come before us and walk with us as we write. Walking the South Downs, I carry the words of many writers — in particular Robert Macfarlane, Anne Wroe, and Gerard Manley Hopkins.

Thank you, Robert Macfarlane, for your guidance along the old ways, for introducing me to Thomas A. Clark and for sharing your word hoard and understanding of the reciprocality of people and landscape with us all.

Thank you, Anne Wroe for illuminating our local landscape, for the poetry and inspiration of *Six Facets of Light*.

The movement and stillness of the work of Richard Long has shaped my thoughts and walks for many years. I hope that we can all walk our own line, make our mark and pass by with the same sense of scale, clarity, commitment and lightness of touch.

This book has been made possible by the vision, tenacity and good humour of Miranda West and the encouragement network of the Do community. Thank you all.

Thanks, too, to designer Wilf Whitty for your skill and agile, easy responses to the book as it shapeshifted.

And thank you to my parents, Helle and Paul Yeates, for sharing their love of walking with me.

I hope that this short tale speaks to a growing collective intention to live with a clearer understanding of our place in the wider community of living beings.

'It is always possible to walk in new ways.' Richard Long

—

Louisa Thomsen Brits lives close to the sea and hills of rural East Sussex, England. She is an author and outdoor swimmer.

Also available

Do Agile Tim Drake

Do Beekeeping Orren Fox

Do Birth Caroline Flint

Do Bitcoin Angelo Morgan-Somers

Do Breathe
Michael Townsend Williams

Do Build Alan Moore

Do Deal
Richard Hoare & Andrew Gummer

Do Death Amanda Blainey

Do Design Alan Moore

Do Disrupt Mark Shayler

Do Drama Lucy Gannon

Do Earth Tamsin Omond

Do Fly Gavin Strange

Do Grow Alice Holden

Do Improvise Robert Poynton

Do Inhabit Sue Fan & Danielle Quigley

Do Lead Les McKeown

Do Listen Bobette Buster

Do Make James Otter

Do Open David Hieatt

Do Pause Robert Poynton

Do Photo Andrew Paynter

Do Present Mark Shayler

Do Preserve
Anja Dunk, Jen Goss & Mimi Beaven

Do Protect Johnathan Rees

Do Purpose David Hieatt

Do Scale Les McKeown

Do Sea Salt
Alison, David & Jess Lea-Wilson

Do Sing James Sills

Do Sourdough Andrew Whitley

Do Start Dan Kieran

Do Story Bobette Buster

Do Team Charlie Gladstone

Do Walk Libby DeLana

Do Wild Baking Tom Herbert

—

The Book of Do *A manual for living*
edited by Miranda West

Path *A short story about reciprocity*
Louisa Thomsen Brits

The Skimming Stone *A short story
about courage* Dominic Wilcox

Stay Curious *How we created a world
class event in a cowshed* Clare Hieatt

The Path of a Doer *A simple tale of
how to get things done* David Hieatt

To hear about events and forthcoming titles, you can find us
on social media @dobookco, or subscribe to our newsletter
via our website: thedobook.co